Doodle Girl

Dear Jacob and Gracie, lots of love xxx
LT

For Paul, H and Phill :)
SS

For Daisy Doo and Betty Boo
MM

SIMON & SCHUSTER
First published in Great Britain in 2017 by Simon & Schuster UK Ltd
1st Floor, 222 Gray's Inn Road, London WC1X 8HB
A CBS Company

Text copyright © 2017 Suzanne Smith & Lindsay Taylor
Illustrations copyright © 2017 Marnie Maurri

The right of Suzanne Smith & Lindsay Taylor to be identified
as the authors and Marnie Maurri as the illustrator of this work
has been asserted by them in accordance with the
Copyright, Designs and Patents Act, 1988

A CIP catalogue record for this book is available from
the British Library upon request

ISBN: 978-1-4711-2319-1
eBook ISBN: 978-1-4711-6870-3

Printed in China
2 4 6 8 10 9 7 5 3 1

Doodle Girl
The Magical Ice Palace

by SUZANNE SMITH & LINDSAY TAYLOR

Illustrated by MARNIE MAURRI

SIMON & SCHUSTER

LONDON   NEW YORK   SYDNEY   TORONTO   NEW DELHI

This is Doodle Girl.

She lives in a **BIG** RED SKETCHBOOK.
But it's not just **ANY** sketchbook.
It's a MaGiC sketchbook.

And Doodle Girl has a
MaGiC PENCIL too.
Whenever she whispers
the words,
"Draw, draw, draw . . ."

AMAZING
ADVENTURES
begin to unfold.

All it takes is a doodle . . .

One day, Doodle Girl was skipping through the sketchbook when she stumbled upon

A curly, CURVY SHAPE.

"Doodling daydreams! Whatever could it be?" said Doodle Girl.

Mr Whizzy and Miss Ladybird
wanted to play . . .

Was it an
UMBRELLA?

Drip!

Drop!

The Small Squeakies were SURE it was CHEESE.
It just HAD to be YUMMY,

scrummy

CHEESE!

Yum!

Yum!

But Doodle Girl had another idea . . .

"Draw, draw, draw,"
she whispered.
And with a D-A-S-H here,
a DOT there and
a swish of her
MaGiC PENCIL,
the curly,
CURVY SHAPE
became
something

BREATHTAKING...

A GIANT **FROSTY SNOWFLAKE!**

"Ta-daa!"
said
Doodle Girl.

"Let's wrap up warm, everyone. It's time for a sparkly adventure . . .

PSSSSSSSKRRRRRROO

The wind BLEW the friends *swirling* and *spinning* over forests

OOOOOO!

and valleys.

They floated

DOWN,

DOWN,

DOWN

until . . .

. . . they landed with a soft **FLUMP** on the **SHIMMERING** snow.

"Brrr!" shivered the Small Squeakies.

"Look at me!" called Doodle Girl, twirling on the ice.

TRUMPETY TOOT!

"Doodling daydreams! Whatever is that noise?" said Doodle Girl.

TRUMPETY TOOT!

"Look up! Look up!"

cried Liddle Birdie.

A HUGE, HAIRY MAMMOTH

was wibbling and wobbling on top of a mountain.

"I think he's stuck!" said Doodle Girl. "We need to help!"

"Draw, draw, draw . . ."
she whispered.

And with a D-A-S-H here,

a DOT there and

a swish of her

MaGiC PENCIL,

she had drawn . . .

"Ooof!" And they all landed on TOP of the Mammoth. Now they could see he was wearing a

SHINY CROWN.

"Oops! Sorry, we didn't mean to land on you. Are you a prince?" asked Doodle Girl.

"YES!" he sniffed sadly. "I sneezed a GINORMOUS SNEEZE and LANDED up here."

"NOW I'm STUCK
and I am going to be LATE
for my PARTY!"
A big tear rolled down
his trunk.

"Oh, please don't cry!"
said Doodle Girl.
"I have an idea . . ."

Quickly, Doodle Girl whispered,
"Draw, draw, draw,"
and with
a D-A-S-H here,
a DOT there and
a swish of her
MAGiC PENCIL,
she drew . . .

BALLOONS!

UP! UP! UP! They all floated high into the sky.

"LOOK! MY ICE PALACE!" pointed the Mammoth. "But how will we get DOWN?"

Doodle Girl winked

at Liddle Birdie . . .

POP! POP! POP!

And with one last POP! they landed outside a <u>beautiful</u> palace.

"Oh! It's your birthday!" said Doodle Girl, spotting the birthday bunting.

"Yes, and you're ALL invited to my PARTY!" said the Mammoth Prince.

"HOORAY!" everyone cried.

Suddenly, the Mammoth let out a GASP . . .

TRUMPETY TOOT!

"OH NO! I forgot the CAKE!

You can't have a party WITHOUT cake!" sobbed the Mammoth Prince.

"Don't worry, I know what to do," reassured Doodle Girl.

"Draw, draw, draw," and with a D-A-S-H here, a DOT there and a SPRINKLING of hundreds and thousands . . .

They all had the most
★ MARVELLOUS ★
TIME.

And with
FULL TUMMIES and
HAPPY SMILES
it was soon time to go back to . . .

...the pages of the **BIG** RED SKETCHBOOK.

Doodle Girl looked at the

curly,
CURVY
SHAPE.

"Now I know what it's for," she said to herself.

With
one last
"Draw, draw, draw, "

she doodled her friends
their very own snow globe
to celebrate their royal adventure.

Happy doodling, everyone!